COSMO girl!

FREAKY DEAKY

150 REALLY SCARY STORIES

FREAKY DEAKY

150 REALLY SCARY STORIES

HEARST BOOKS

A division of Sterling Publishing Co., Inc.

New York / London
www.sterlingpublishing.com

Book design by Margaret Rubiano

Library of Congress Cataloging-in-Publication Data is available

10 9 8 7 6 5 4 3 2 1

Published by Hearst Books
A Division of Sterling Publishing Co., Inc.
387 Park Avenue South, New York, NY 10016

CosmoGIRL! and Hearst Books are trademarks
of Hearst Communications, Inc.

www.cosmogirl.com

For information about custom editions, special sales,
premium and corporate purchases, please contact Sterling
Special Sales Department at 800-805-5489 or
specialsales@sterlingpublishing.com.

Distributed in Canada by Sterling Publishing
C/o Canadian Manda Group, 165 Dufferin Street
Toronto, Ontario, Canada M6K 3H6

Distributed in Australia by Capricorn Link (Australia) Pty. Ltd.
P.O. Box 704, Windsor, NSW 2756 Australia

Manufactured in China

Sterling ISBN: 978-1-58816-672-2

Illustration credits:
Kareem Iliya Pages 20, 34, 48, 62, 68, 74, 80, 94, 102, 118,
124, 132, 150, 166, 184.
Richard May Page 110.
Yuko Shimizu Page 10, 54, 142.
Sam Weber Page 5, 24, 38, 86, 158, 174, 192.

Hey CosmoGIRL!s,

A few years back we started a column in *CosmoGIRL!* magazine that let you tell us about your experiences with the supernatural. You sent us stories about things that have happened to you that seem to have no explanation—dreams you've had that turned out to predict actual future occurrences, pets with a sixth sense who knew when you were in danger and took you out of harm's way, and even times when you felt like you've been contacted by loved ones who've passed away. Because these stories all give us chills, we called the column "Freaky Deaky." And it's been one of our most popular features! I think it's because all of us have experienced those moments when we feel like we've stepped into a third dimension. You see, you CosmoGIRL!s are very intuitive people—whether you're religious or spiritual, the fact is, you tend to listen to your own sixth sense. You know that you don't always have to see something to believe it. Sometimes, you just get a *feeling*, right? And listening to those feelings helps you understand yourself and helps guide you through your life. So when you say you think your Grandmother was sending you a message from heaven or that you just *know* your dog Fletcher saved your life? You know those people who roll their eyes about it? Well, I feel sorry for them! Because I, for one, believe in those special moments, and that's why those stories not only go in the magazine, but now you have a collection of them. I hope this book inspires you to welcome those "freaky deaky" moments in your own life.

So keep this book by your bed and when something like this happens to you, be sure to let me know about it, okay? I'm here for you at susan@cosmogirl.com.

Love,

Susan

boo tube

" My mom and I were staying in a hotel one night, when the person in the room next door turned up the volume on the TV as loud as it could go. We were annoyed, so we called the front desk to complain. They said no one had checked in to that room, but they'd call just in case. We could hear the phone ringing through the wall, but no one picked up. Then the manager came up and listened through the wall. He even checked all of the rooms surrounding ours, but they were all empty! The noise from the TV finally went away, but we were so freaked out that we switched rooms anyway. And we're definitely never going to stay there again! **"**

double trouble

" I was hanging out at my friend's house one night. There was a board game sitting out, so I grabbed the dice and started to roll them. The first time, they landed on doubles. I rolled again—and *again*—and got doubles each time! I thought I was going crazy, so I told my friend to try. She thinks that her house is haunted, so she said, 'If there are any ghosts here, let the dice read doubles again.' And she rolled doubles! It happened two more times until finally we got two different numbers. It may have been a coincidence, but still, it was the weirdest thing *ever*! "

hell-evator

" Last year, I spent a semester in Korea, where they have late-night cram sessions in the dorms. One night, I headed back to my room on the 22nd floor of my building around 2:00 a.m. It was pitch black as I made my way to the elevator and hit the button. The elevator began to go up, but then it stopped at the 5th floor. The doors opened but no one came in. The elevator then stopped at the 12th *and* the 18th floor—and again, no one was there. The next thing I knew, the 'maximum weight' alarm began to ring and I ran out of that elevator, up the stairs, and into my dorm room. I immediately changed my cram sessions to the afternoons! "

cat call

" Two years ago, my dad passed away suddenly. The night before his funeral, I was crying hysterically on my back porch. As I cried, I said, 'Daddy, I just want to see you one more time, just for five more minutes,' wishing that he could hear me. Then this black cat came out of the woods and walked right up to me. He was purring, and I started petting him. About five minutes later, the cat just got up and left. The thing is, my dad always said that if reincarnation really existed, he'd want to come back as a black cat! So I'm *positive* it was him! **"**

sprite-mare

"Once I dreamed that I was lying in a bed with other people and they kept touching me in random places and purring. They looked exactly how my grandma had described fairies. Before she died she'd talked about how fairies were leaving handprints on her. She said they had razor-sharp teeth and these black eyes that looked like shining orbs. In my dream two of the fairies held me down and the others began cutting me with knives. Blood was somehow all over the walls as if it was squirting from my cuts. Then one of them suddenly put a hand on my face and I stopped breathing. I woke up shaking and sweating."

dream boy

" A few weeks ago, I had a really strange dream. In it, I was walking to my school bus. As I crossed the street, a huge truck came out of nowhere and whizzed by me without even slowing down. Then this quiet boy who always waits with me got hit by the truck. I woke up right after and didn't think much about it until two mornings later. I was about to cross the street to get on my bus and I wasn't really paying attention, so I stepped off the curb without looking. But then the same guy who was in my dream suddenly grabbed my arm. I stopped to see what he wanted, and he just told me to watch out—roaring past us was a huge truck. The driver just flew right by us, ignoring the stop sign on our bus! I would have been hit if it weren't for him! It totally creeps me out knowing that the boy I saw get hit in my dream actually saved me from the same fate in real life. **"**

bad car-ma

" One night, my friend and I were out driving around town on a back road that crossed over some train tracks. As we were approaching the tracks, we saw headlights from a car in front of us. We crossed the tracks and kept following the road, and suddenly the headlights completely disappeared! There was nowhere for the car to turn off, and we had clearly seen the lights—we had no idea where it had gone. Later we found out that a man had died when his car was hit by a train on those same tracks 10 years ago. Now, I'm always leery about going anywhere near those tracks! "

scaredy cat

" A couple of weeks after my cat, Whiskers, passed away, I heard a few faint meows coming from my dining room. It was late at night, so I just told myself that I was imagining things, and I ignored it. The next night, I was reading in my den when Whiskers's favorite toy rolled out from the dining room. I got so freaked out that I ran upstairs and went right to my room! I was almost too scared to believe it. But in a way, it's a little comforting knowing that Whiskers is still around— at least in spirit! "

help from above

" One day I accidentally left my house key at school. Since nobody was home and my parents were going to be at work for a few more hours, I was stuck. I tried everything I could to get the door open—jiggling the knob and even sticking a bobby pin in the lock—but nothing was working. I was so frustrated about being locked out that I started to cry. Then I thought of my grandfather, who had died the year before. When he was alive, he always helped me out of jams. So I closed my eyes and said, 'Grandpa, if you really love me, will you help me out and open this door?' Then I turned the knob again and the door came right open! I haven't told this to anyone because I don't think they will believe me—but it really did happen! **"**

angel song

❝ Right after my uncle Bobby died, we were looking through some photos when my aunt picked up a music box he had given her. Music never came from it unless it was open. Well, the box was closed, but all of a sudden, it started to play. My aunt opened and closed it several times, but it wouldn't stop. Then she thought it might be a sign from Bobby telling us he was okay, so she said, 'Bobby, please stop the music. I don't want to have to break this.' And the music stopped. I think it was his way of saying hi. ❞

sharp instincts

" Last year, as I was riding
in the backseat of my
dad's car on the way to
the store, I noticed that
one of my fingernails had
chipped. I got my metal nail file out of
my purse to fix it. As I began to file, a
strong urge came over me to put it
away, quickly. So I dropped the file
back into my purse. Seconds later, the
woman driving behind us smashed into
the back of our car. I went flying forward
and crashed into the passenger seat in
front of me. I was totally fine, but I can
only imagine what would have happened
if I had still been using that supersharp
nail file when she hit us! "

psychic
powers

point taken

" Just days before my grandpa died on a cruise, he bought my grandma an expensive tea set. He wasn't happy about buying it because it cost so much, but my grandma really wanted it. After he died, my grandma was too sad to look at the tea set, so she put it on the top shelf in her garage. One day I was at her house and heard a crash coming from the garage. I went in to see what had happened, and the tea set was shattered in pieces on the floor. My grandma doesn't have pets and no one had been in the garage at the time, so I know it was my grandfather proving a point. Guess he *really* didn't want that tea set! "

savannahhhh!

" Once I went on a ghost tour of Savannah, Georgia. Our guide told us about a woman who was sentenced to death after murdering her husband to be with her true love. The woman was pregnant, so she was allowed to have the baby, but it was taken away right before she was hanged. Now, hundreds of years later, they say that you can sometimes hear the woman crying, or that she'll follow you around the square, thinking you have her baby. After the tour, I was standing in the square when I felt a tug on the back of my shirt and someone was pulling hard on my hair. But when I turned around, no one was there! "

tapped in

" My brother died in a car accident three years ago. Recently, our bathroom sink tap started turning on whenever someone was in the shower. It happened to my mom first, but she just thought it was my sister or me coming in and leaving it on. Then the faucet started to turn on when my sister or I would be taking a shower *with the door locked.* And it wasn't like the tap was just drizzling—it was on full blast! The weird thing is, when my brother was alive he had a habit of forgetting to turn off the tap after he used it. My dad is a mechanic and he said there was no way the water could come on without someone turning the handle. We have since modernized the taps and the mysterious running water doesn't happen anymore. Still, it makes you wonder...**"**

strange brew

❝ We were up at our cabin one summer and my grandma wanted to take me to an antique store. While we were there, I bought a tea set. The lady at the counter put all the pieces in a basket and told me it had come from an abandoned house. When we got back to the cabin, I locked the basket for safekeeping while we were away and put it on my dresser. A couple of weeks later we went to stay at our cabin again. When I looked in my room, the tea basket had been opened and two tea glasses had been left on my art desk with a little bit of tea in them! ❞

brace yourself

" My friend taught me how to make these 'magic' string bracelets. You're supposed to make a wish before tying it around your wrist, and when it falls off, the wish will come true. When I tied mine on, I wished that my crush and his girlfriend would break up. A few days later, my bracelet fell off. The next morning at school, I passed my crush on the way to class and noticed that he looked upset. I asked him what was wrong, and he told me that his girlfriend had cheated on him and they'd broken up! My friend and I were totally freaked out—and we never told a soul about the bracelet! "

mr. sunshine

" My mom was having an awful day, and she had to take my brother and sister and me to the dentist. When we got there, an older man was sitting in the waiting room. He started talking to us, telling us jokes, and he even read my little sister a book. Eventually, the man said his goodbyes, grabbed his hat, and left. My mom wanted to tell him how much he had brightened her bad day, but when we went outside, there were no cars leaving the parking lot and we didn't see him walking anywhere. We stepped outside literally seconds after he did, but he was nowhere in sight! Every time I think of that man, I get the chills—I seriously believe he was an angel sent to my mother on her horrible day. **"**

wedding crasher

" Last year, I was a junior bridesmaid at my sister's wedding. While we were helping her get ready for the ceremony in her hotel room, I caught a glimpse of a guy who looked just like her old boyfriend who had died three years earlier. At first I tried not to think about it so I could focus on the wedding. But then at the reception, I saw the guy again—this time he was looking at my sister and smiling before he disappeared. I've had nightmares about him ever since, but I haven't told anyone about this because I don't want to scare my sister! "

ghostly encounter

night *dive*

" In my dream, my school was flooded, and there were fish, stingrays, and small sharks swimming in the water. I was trying to swim out toward the doors. I had to get up to the surface to take a breath, but I couldn't make it to the top. I needed air so badly that I woke up and I couldn't breathe. I had been holding my breath in my sleep! I lay there panicking for about four seconds until I sat up and started breathing really hard. **"**

alarm-ing news

" My brother Patrick died nine years ago, and we always visit his grave on his birthday. One time, I left a card for him that said, 'Please show us a sign that you got this.' When we got home, we were just sitting around when all of a sudden, our smoke alarm went off— even though we weren't cooking or doing anything involving smoke. The password to turn off the alarm? Patrick! It was exactly the sign I'd asked for. "

house guest

" In the first year after my dad died, all sorts of weird things started to happen around my house. I would hear his beer cans opening and him saying, 'Oh, Jessica,' just like he always used to. The freakiest thing that happened was when I was reading in our living room alone, and the TV suddenly turned on to a New York Giants game—his favorite team! I know I wasn't going crazy because my mom was experiencing strange things too. I guess it was just my dad's way of saying hi. "

killer instinct

psychic powers

" On my 13th birthday, I was watching my older brother ride around on his four-wheeler. He needed to get a shovel from the shed across the road, and he asked me if I wanted to come along. I didn't have a helmet with me and a gut feeling told me not to go, so I stayed there and watched him drive off. On his way back, he pulled out in front of a truck and was hit so hard, the four-wheeler flipped over and he went flying. He was okay, but the police said that if I had been with him, I would have been killed. I'm so glad I listened to my instincts and didn't go with him that day! "

armed & dangerous

" One night I dreamed that I was walking along this path in the woods by my house and suddenly a guy reached out and grabbed my wrist. When I looked at him, he had on this really scary mask, and I woke up screaming. Then I looked at my wrist, and there was a handprint right where he had grabbed me in my dream! I don't know what happened that night, but I was totally freaked out and couldn't go back to sleep. "

window watcher

" When I was little, my grandmother used to always tell me, 'There's a nice little girl ghost who lives in this house. Go outside to your tree house and watch the windows because she likes to look outside a lot.' I would spend all day in the tree house watching, but I never saw anything. Now my little sister plays in the tree house. I was in there with her recently when I saw a little girl peering out from one of the windows of my grandmother's house! I got so scared and ran to my grandmother. She smiled and said, 'No one else believed me!' Ever since, I've been too spooked to go there. "

nuts & bolt

"One night I went to my aunt's house to sleep over. Her house is old, and the room that I slept in has a door that leads to the attic stairs. Around two in the morning the doorknob to the attic started to jiggle, like someone was turning it on the other side. I froze, pulled my covers over my head, and didn't move. It stopped for a while, and I calmed down, thinking that I was just tired and hallucinating. But then it started again, except this time it was louder. I was so scared! I leapt out of bed and ran to my cousin's room to sleep for the rest of the night. I will never sleep in that room again!"

student body

"On the first day of school last year, I was sitting in math class and the teacher was talking to us about our homework. All of a sudden I heard a girl's voice behind me say, 'Get out of my seat, you idiot.' I turned around but there wasn't anyone sitting behind me. Then I heard it again. She said, 'I told you to get out of my seat, okay?' I turned around for the second time,

ghostly encounter

but still no one was there. After school I told the teacher about what I'd heard because I thought it was so weird. She said, 'Oh, yes. A girl who was in my class two years ago got hit by a car. She used to sit in your seat. Sometimes kids say they can hear her voice. But don't worry, she won't do anything to you.' Luckily I haven't heard her voice since, but I'm still creeped out! **"**

sound decision

" One night I was home alone waiting for my mom to get off work. She usually gets home around midnight, but that night she was running late. I was in bed, and at 12:30 I heard the door downstairs open and someone start walking upstairs. I assumed it was my mom. When she reached my room, she was having trouble with the doorknob, so I got up and opened the door—but my mom wasn't there! No one was there! I freaked out and called her name, but there was no response. So I called her cell phone to ask where she was, and she said she'd be home in 10 minutes! I was so scared that I ran downstairs and waited for her outside. "

early show

" I had to get up around 5 a.m. one day to go to the state fair. I was running around getting ready when I noticed something move in my computer room. I stopped to see what it was, and I saw a guy in the window. I was so shocked! He was pale and had on a big hat. Then I blinked and he was gone. What's weird is that I was on the second floor, so he couldn't have been standing outside. Now I always make sure the blinds are closed at night. "

petal pusher

" One night I was at my grandmother's house and she was telling me stories about weird stuff that happens there, like she hears things fall off tables when she's the only one home. She's convinced that someone died in the house before she moved in. I didn't really get worked up about it, but around midnight that night, I woke up. I could've sworn that I'd heard something fall in the kitchen. I got

up and went to ask my cousin if she'd
heard the sound too. She said that she
had. So we got up our nerve and went
to the kitchen together to check it out.
We looked around and saw that a vase
of flowers that was on the table had
fallen onto the floor. But the weird
thing was that when we'd all gone to
bed the flowers had been sitting in
the middle of the table. I was
completely spooked! **"**

going postal

" My grandfather made us a mailbox that looked like our house. After he died, we were moving to a new place, and we bought a replacement mailbox so we could bring his with us. At first, my dad wasn't going to switch them right away, but I got very upset and cried until he did. That night, a drunk driver crashed into the new box and totally destroyed it. My grandfather's was safe in our basement. Somehow, I had this feeling that we just had to take down his mailbox that day. "

camp fear

" There was a legend about the man who used to own my summer camp. His name was Crazy Joe. The story is that if you say that you don't believe in him out loud while you're on the campground, he'll come after you. So one summer the girls from my bunk and I were on a hayride in the woods and we drove right past Crazy Joe's old house. While we were talking about him one girl yelled out, 'I don't believe in Crazy Joe!' Then moments later a tree fell right in front of our tractor, trapping us in the woods for hours. Now I definitely believe that Crazy Joe is real! "

out cold

psychic powers

" One morning I was walking into my high school when I was overcome by a horrible sense of dread. It stopped me dead in my tracks. My friends asked me what was wrong, but I didn't know how to explain it. The bell rang, so we hurried to class. Later I was called to the office and told that my parents were picking me up. I found out that my grandmother had died at 8:32 that morning. The school bell rings at 8:30—right when I'd felt so strange. Thinking about it now still gives me chills. "

night light

" I wasn't feeling well one night,
and my room was really hot, so
I went to sleep in the living room.
At about 1 a.m., I woke up to go to
the bathroom and get a drink.
When I opened my eyes, I was
staring at my parents' door. I looked
again and saw the outline of a man
in a golden light standing there right
in front of their door. He had no real

features; it was just an outline of him. I watched him a moment as he sort of glided over toward my brother's room and went inside. Then I got up and went over to see if the man was in there. But when I opened the door, my brother was just lying in bed, sound asleep, and there was no sign of anything!**"**

jaw dropper

" I had a dream that I was sucked into the shower drain and men with yellow eyes and long chins were chasing me. They wanted me to be their queen. I don't know what was going to happen because I woke up just as they were about to grab me. It was really weird! "

sketchy night

" I was having trouble sleeping one night, so I was looking out my window. Suddenly I saw a guy walk past. He turned and looked at me and I freaked out! I'm a pretty good artist, so I got up and sketched everything I could remember about him. I posted my drawing all over the neighborhood, hoping to find out if anyone knew him. One of my neighbors called to say that the guy I'd seen was the previous owner of my house—he had died in there because his wife had killed him! My family searched for his picture online. Sure enough, it looked just like him. Ever since then, I have been so scared! "

floor show

"My sister and I share a room and I sleep on the top of our bunk beds. My closet, which has mirrored doors, is directly across from my bed. One night I thought I heard my computer turn on. Since I'm up so high, I usually look in the mirror to see what's going on. But that night, when I checked out the reflection, I saw what appeared to be my sister sitting on the floor, so I said, 'Stephanie, what the heck are you doing?' Then I leaned over to look at her, but she was asleep in her bed! I glanced back at the reflection in the mirror, and the girl was still there! I had a hard time sleeping that night!"

family fuse

" My Uncle Jimmy passed away three years ago in March. He'd been living with my grandparents in Virginia when he died, and my grandfather says that Jimmy's presence has been visiting their house ever since. I just went along with it, though I never actually thought it was true. But last summer I flew to Virginia as part of my graduation present. My first night there, Papa said, 'Jimmy is here,' and the lights flickered! I was so freaked out, but I thought it might be a coincidence so I shrugged it off. Then the next night Papa said, 'Wasn't that nice of Jimmy to come around last night?' and the lights flickered again! I know nobody else in the house could've done it because my grandma was upstairs sleeping and Papa is in a wheelchair and wasn't anywhere near the light switch. I am now convinced that my uncle really is there in spirit! "

flower girl

ghostly encounter

" I went to visit my great-grandmother's grave one day. While I was 'talking' to my gran, I suddenly heard a little girl laughing. It sounded like she was quite close to me, but I was alone. I looked around, and even though there was no wind, the flowers on the grave next to my great-grandmother's were rustling. I walked over and read the tombstone. It belonged to a little girl! "

how biz-czar!

" Ever since I was in fifth grade I've had dreams about being Maria Romanov, the third daughter of the last czar of Russia. I have had countless visions, memories, and many dreams of my past life. Once I had a nightmare of being shot in the side and the thigh (supposedly Maria was shot to death). When I woke up, I felt pressure in those areas. Freaky! Plus, in my dreams I see my royal sisters playing cards and swimming at the beach. I've had too many dreams to write here, and some too hard to explain, but I know I was her. My parents say they believe me, but I doubt it. I've only told my closest friends about my connection to the Romanov family. They think it's weird. "

landing pad

"Okay, this is going to sound crazy, but it's really true! One night, my family was asleep when the whole house started shaking—but the weird thing is, we live in a place where there are never earthquakes. I screamed and ran into my parents' room, and as we waited for the shaking to stop, an eerie light came in from the backyard. We looked out but didn't see anything. Then it all stopped as fast as it had started. The next day, my dad found four large round dents in our grass. I don't know about anyone else, but I so believe in aliens now!"

team spirit

"" My dad manages an arena and one
night I was helping him close it. We
started by locking all the doors
upstairs, then we went to the doors
downstairs. Out of nowhere this old guy
walked up to us and asked if there was
a hockey game going on. My dad told
him that he had to leave because the
arena was closed. The man left. Then
30 minutes later, when we were about
to go home, the man came walking
down the stairs from the top part of

the building. My dad asked him how he had gotten in, and he said through the door upstairs. But every door upstairs was locked! Once again my dad told the man to leave. This time he left through the front door, where I was standing. I was watching him walk away when I looked at my dad for a second, then I looked back out the door. The man was gone! I freak out every time I think about that night. **"**

shower radio

"One night I came home and saw a note from my parents that said they wouldn't be home until later. I decided to take a shower. Since no one was home I set my radio on the bathroom counter and blasted my music. About 10 minutes later, there was a knock on the bathroom door. I was startled, but I heard the door open and what sounded like my mom say, 'Hi, honey, we're home. I'm just turning your music down a little,' and it seemed like she did. Well, when I got out of the shower my parents were nowhere to be found! I called my mom's cell and asked her where she was. She had never been home because she was sitting in a restaurant with my dad!"

stab in the dark

"One night I had a dream that I was in Ottawa, Canada, and I was going to meet my mom. The place where we were supposed to meet was closed, so I went to a run-down grocery store nearby. I asked to use the phone and the lady at the counter said, 'There is no need to call. Your mom is dead. She was stabbed until there was no more life left in her.' I immediately woke up. It was around 5:30 in the morning, so I got up and I found my mom in the kitchen. She told me that she had had the weirdest dream where she was in a big house in Ottawa and I had been stabbed. For the rest of the week it took me twice as long as normal to get to sleep."

gray area

" I was home alone watching TV one night when I saw a moving shadow. I walked around the corner to see what it was. When I did, I saw a man wearing a gray hat with a red feather. I freaked and ran to my room! Two days later I was cleaning the coat closet and I found that exact gray hat. I asked my mom whose it was. She said it had belonged to my grandfather, who died before I was born. On his deathbed he had touched her stomach and said, 'This one is going to be an athlete.' And I am! "

walkie talkie

" One really windy day I was walking to my friend's house when I heard someone call my name. I turned around to see who it was, but no one was there. I kept walking until I heard someone call my name again and say, 'Stop, don't go any farther.' The voice sounded like it was right in my ear! I stopped, and suddenly I heard a big crash. About 5 feet in front of me a tree blew over from the wind. I was creeped out! "

shout out

" I was alone in my room one night and I played a song on my computer that I know the lyrics to. Suddenly I heard a woman scream, 'Let me out!' It was crystal clear and it came from my computer. I freaked and unplugged the computer. No one took me seriously, but I know what I heard. "

free bird

" My parents were out of town on the day of my friend Felicia's funeral and I was freaking out because I didn't have a ride. I was trying to call my friend Sarah, who also knew Felicia, but I couldn't remember her number. I sat down by my phone and started to cry because I was afraid I wasn't going to make it to the funeral. Then all of a sudden a white bird flew down and

started to tap on my window. Suddenly
a random phone number came to me
and I dialed it. I was shocked when I
heard Sarah's mom on the other end.
Later, at the funeral, I was talking to
Felicia's parents and they told me that
a white bird was sitting on their porch
earlier that day too. Now every time
I see a white bird, I look at it a
lot differently. **"**

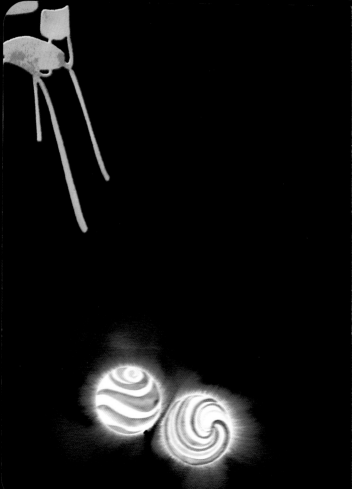

marble floors

" My older brother was moving into a spooky old house. While I was helping him carry boxes, I saw two marbles at the top of his stairs. Not thinking much of it, I picked them up and set them on a table. Over the next two weeks my brother and I found a dozen marbles in random places like the middle of the living room and in doorways. A month later, at my brother's housewarming party, I told his friend about the marbles. She didn't believe me until she looked down and saw two marbles on the kitchen floor! We still don't know where the marbles are coming from, but they keep appearing all over the house. **"**

creepaway camp

"I went to a leadership camp last September, and on my first night there I didn't sleep well. I kept waking up, feeling like someone was shaking me, and I thought I heard voices. I'd sit up in bed and the room would look like it was filled with smoke, yet I could breathe perfectly. When I woke up the next morning, I asked if anyone else in my cabin had slept restlessly and they said no, so I dismissed the whole thing. But later, after we came home, my friends from camp and I were swapping pictures, and in every picture that had been taken outside of our cabin, there were three orbs. And we had all used different cameras! It was so strange."

tribal instincts

"One night I had a dream that I was in an African savannah—a grassy flatland. I saw some people hunting antelope and I ran to join them, but I couldn't catch up. Suddenly, a tiger jumped in front of me and said, 'Princess!' Then I woke up. A few days later my mom pulled out some of our old home videos and I started to watch one from when I was little. As I watched it, my 4-year-old self said, 'There was a tiger when I was a princess in Africa...' I'm now convinced that I was an African princess in a past life!"

milking it

" One night I was asleep in my room and suddenly I heard the voice of a girl who I thought was my sister. She said, 'Isha, can you give me some milk?' (Isha is my nickname.) I told her it was too late for milk, and she said, 'No, please!' So I decided to get up. But when I pulled the covers down, there was no one there. I went to my sister's room but she wasn't there, so I went to my parents' room. My mom was watching television and next to her was my sister—fast asleep! I thought I had dreamed the entire thing. Then, less than two months later, my aunt came to visit and slept in my room. I hadn't told her the story, but that night she woke me up and told me that she could have sworn my sister had held her hand and woke her up because she wanted some milk. Again, my sister was in my parents' bedroom. My aunt was so freaked out, she couldn't sleep. Creepy, isn't it? **"**

night prowler

"One night I went to bed and fell asleep right away. The next thing I knew, I was standing over my own body watching myself sleep. Then I walked all through my house. I even went outside and walked around my neighborhood. When I woke up in the morning, I figured it must have been a dream. But my neighbor said he saw me walking around the street at 3 a.m. It was creepy beyond all belief!"

plane scary

" One night I dreamed that I was sitting on a plane next to my mom and her face started falling off! I looked around the plane and everyone else's faces were falling off too! They were saying my name over and over again, and then the plane started crashing down. I didn't know what to do so I screamed. Then I woke up crying. "

forever young

" My grandmother and I have the same birthday, but she died before I was born, so I never met her. My mom thinks we have a special connection. She tells me I have her hand gestures and nervous habits. When I was little, a meeting with my aunt proved that my mom's theory was true. My Aunt Ruth came to visit for the first time, and the second I saw her I called her Jacky, as if I knew her really well. I found out later that Jacky is my aunt's middle name, but my grandmother used it like a nickname! I don't call her Jacky now because it hits a sensitive spot, but I still get the urge to every time I see her! "

moving pictures

" My dad found some historical paintings the people before us had left in the basement and hung them up down there. One was of a weird man with a feathered hat and a big beard that just gave me the creeps. I begged my dad to throw it out, but he wouldn't. One night, as we slept, there was a huge crash. It turns out the painting fell down, so my dad fixed it. A few weeks later, I was home alone when I heard another crash. I ran to my room to wait for my parents. When they got home, my dad went downstairs, figuring the portrait fell again—but this time, he didn't see it anywhere. It mysteriously disappeared! He thinks I threw it out, but I swear I didn't. But I'll admit—I'm glad it's gone. **"**

gnaw-ty girl

"I always have dreams where I'm a rat. Then, when I actually wake up, I'm usually in the kitchen nibbling on food like a rat. I haven't told anyone this before because I'm afraid they'll think I'm going insane, but I have a weird feeling that my dreams come from my past life as a rodent."

afterlife of the party

" At my graduation party I was showing my grandmother what we had done to my room since we started remodeling it. As we were walking out, I glanced in the mirror and saw my grandfather sitting on my bed. When I looked a second time, he wasn't there. Then later on, my brother's friend was walking through the living room and went to the

ghostly encounter

bathroom. When he came back he turned to my brother and said, 'There was this guy sitting on your couch when I went into the bathroom, but he wasn't there when I came out and I haven't seen him anywhere else.' When my brother asked him what the man looked like, his friend pointed to a picture of my grandfather on the wall. My grandfather passed away last May, but it looks like he still made an appearance at my party! "

who's there?

" One day I was in my room talking on the phone to my friend Amanda when I heard a loud knock on my wall. I thought it was just my little brother being his annoying self, because my room is right next to his. So I knocked right back, and he responded by knocking again. I tried knocking several times so I could outdo him, but he did the same exact thing back. I had to get off the phone with my friend so I could go strangle my brother, but when I got to his room, he wasn't there. I thought he was hiding somewhere. But then I saw him downstairs with my mom baking cookies. He was never in his room! Creepy! **"**

study buddy

" It was a Tuesday night and I was talking on instant messenger when someone IMed me with the screen name UrFuTuRe221, saying I should go study my vocabulary words for English class. I ignored it and kept IMing, but then the next day my English teacher gave us a vocabulary pop quiz! Guess what? I failed! So after school, I tried to IM UrFuTuRe221, but I got an error message: 'Nobody by that username exists.' Now I wish I had paid attention to the message. Whenever I think about that night, I get the chills! "

sixth sense

❝I had just started my new job when I met a strange coworker. He was nice—that is, when he managed to get more than two words out. On our first meeting, he told me, 'She's very pretty.' I thought he meant me, so I said, 'Thank you.' About a month after that, he walked up to me and asked, 'Is she loud?' I didn't know what he was talking about, so I said, 'Who?' He asked again, and when I responded that I had no idea who he was talking about, he stared at me blankly and said, 'Your mother. She's yelling at you right now. She's standing next to you with two other presences. Men. One's much older. She's still trying to tell you...' That's all he could get out before I started crying hysterically. I had never told anyone at my new job that I lost both my parents and my grandpa about five years earlier. There's no way he could have possibly known."

what a doll

"After my aunt died, my dad gave me a Native American doll that had been hers. One day I was showing it to my friend and I put it by my bed. Out of nowhere, my dog started barking at it. He got annoying, so we moved the doll. He followed it, still barking! We freaked out and took the doll into the living room, and finally he stopped barking. Later, my mom told me that ghosts follow their belongings. Now I always keep that doll where I can see it!"

blue clues

ghostly encounter

" I was home alone watching TV one night when my show cut out. After waiting for the show to come back on, I got bored. I went upstairs and realized the power in my room was off, but it didn't seem to be off anywhere else in the house. I went into my parents' bedroom to see if they had electricity, and came face to face with a ghost! She had a pale, bluish face with hair blowing across it. Her eyes were hollow. I'm positive I saw her. The next day, I overheard my parents talking about the owners of the house before us. It turned out the wife mysteriously disappeared one night in 1982. Freaky, huh? "

dead ringer

" One night at around 2 o'clock in the morning, I heard the doorbell ringing like crazy. Half asleep, I got up and turned on the lights in the hallway and went to the door. When I looked through the peephole, I saw my friend Jared, so I opened the door right away. But when I looked outside, nobody was there. The weird thing was that Jared had passed away a couple of weeks earlier. None of it hit me until the morning, when I was telling my mom what had happened. She said I was probably just dreaming, but all of the lights were still on from when I had turned them on the night before! **"**

grand intuition

" A couple of years ago, right after my grandma died, I had a dream that there was a strange man in my basement. When I woke up, it was the middle of the night, and I saw a figure that looked like my grandma standing by my bed. She was pointing to my dad's room, so I went in there and woke him up. I told him my dream about the man in the basement and

ghostly encounter

that I had seen Grandma in my room. He decided to go see if there really was anyone in the basement. He turned on the light in the stairwell and noticed that the side door was unlocked, and there were muddy footprints on the floor. We never knew who was down there, but my dad still thanks me for waking him up that night. I don't know what would have happened to us if I hadn't had that dream. **"**

pop eye

" This may not sound true, but I swear it is. I was at a contact lens demonstration with my friend and her mom. My friend couldn't get the contacts in because she kept closing her eye right before she let go of the contact. So her mom was showing her how to hold her lower eyelid to put the contact in, and her eyelid got stuck behind her eyeball! It was the scariest thing I had ever seen in my life. Her eye looked like the size of a golf ball. I could've sworn it was going to fall out of her head. Ew! **"**

extra freaky

wall power

" I was about to go to sleep when I noticed that my mom had hung these porcelain masks on my wall. I had told her earlier that I didn't like them. They were freaky-looking! But she insisted, and hung them by the ribbons that were attached to the back of them. In the middle of the night I heard a muffled crash. I thought it was just the thunder outside, so I continued to sleep. When I woke up in the morning, I looked where the masks had been and saw that they were on the floor in pieces. The nails that went through the ribbons were still in my wall, but the ribbons themselves were nowhere to be seen. "

bye-bye birdie

" When my grandma died, she left me her bird, Sarge. The coolest thing about Sarge was that he used to say, 'Honey, I'm home!'—but *only* when my grandma walked into the room. Well, one night when I was falling asleep in my room all alone with Sarge, out of nowhere he suddenly said, 'Honey, I'm home!' It scared me so bad that I had to sleep in the living room for the rest of the night. Now I make sure Sarge stays in the kitchen! **"**

furnishing touches

" Last summer my parents and I went on vacation to France and we stayed in this really old stone hotel. Our room was sort of like an attic. One evening my mom woke up in the middle of the night and noticed that one of the chairs had been moved close to the side of the bed. She just moved it back and didn't think anything of it. Then, in the morning, we noticed that the big wooden dresser had moved in a diagonal line three feet away from the wall. When we looked at the wall behind where the dresser had been, there was a small door. We tried to open it, but it was locked tight. Just then, the door to our room blew wide open! We asked to change rooms, but the hotel was full, so we had to stay in that creepy place! 🙶

just my type

psychic powers

" I have this weird habit: When I get bored, I picture a keyboard in my mind and imagine typing the same random word over and over again on it. So one day during class I was sitting next to this really quiet girl who barely ever speaks. I was just daydreaming of that keyboard and typing 'Brody' in my mind (you can guess who I have a crush on), when all of a sudden I heard her saying 'Brody' over and over. She kept muttering to herself, and when I asked her if she was okay, she jumped like she was being woken up from a dream. "

running cold

" My sister and I were at our dad's cottage. I was clearing the dinner table when I heard a funny noise coming from the bathroom. The door was open a little bit, and I could see the mirror but nothing else. All of a sudden I heard this big thud and then a squeak coming from inside the bathroom. I thought it was just the wind or some animal outside, but then I heard water running. I got my dad to go investigate because I was scared someone was in there. I followed behind him, and when we went in, the cold water tap was running! The window was locked and the blinds were down, so no one had gotten in, but it sure felt like someone was there! "

abby-normal

" I had just moved into this house in Maine that is over 100 years old. Many people say that it's haunted. One night the stars were really bright, so everyone went stargazing. I decided to go home early, and when I was walking back to the house, I saw this dog that seemed transparent. It was sitting on a big rock right next to my house, looking out to the road. The next day I went to lunch with my mom and the man who lived in the house before us. We were looking at pictures, and one of them was of a dog that looked like the one on the rock! I didn't even have to ask questions, because right when he saw it he said, 'Oh! That was my dog, Abby. She used to love to sit on the big rock next to the house and look out onto the road.'**"**

shagadelic!

" One day we got our carpet shampooed, and it was raked so that it all lay one way. Then the carpet guy, my mom, and I all left through the kitchen door. When we got home later, there was a line of footprints leading to my room (which is not in the direction of the kitchen). But instead of a set, it was just one foot, like someone had hopped! I was freaked; so was my mom. She told me that I used to have an imaginary friend and when she'd asked me what the friend looked like, I'd said, 'She has black hair, blue eyes, and one leg.' "

sound check

" I went to stay at my grandma's house for the summer. She has an upstairs bedroom that my mom would stay in. One day I had to go clean out the closet in that room and organize some clothes. After I was done, I lay across the bed because I was really tired. Suddenly, I heard a noise that sounded like the radio going through a bunch of different channels and static. It scared me crapless because I knew no one had been up in that room for a very long time and I never played the radio while I was cleaning. I didn't move while I was lying on the bed. Finally, after a few seconds, it stopped. When I went to check out what was wrong with the radio, the switch was off. What was even more creepy was that the cord was unplugged from the socket (and the radio isn't battery operated). After a few months, when I had gone back to school, my grandma's house burned down for some unknown reason that the police and firemen couldn't identify. Eek! **"**

the electric slide

extra freaky

" I was singing into my friend's karaoke machine one night when everything went black. Then, suddenly, I was walking down a tunnel toward a light. But before I got to the light, I woke up in a hospital bed! The doctors told me I'd been shocked by the machine and had arrived with no pulse. I was supposedly dead for a few minutes, but they saved me! "

in-tall-erable cruelty

" For some odd reason I've always felt uncomfortable around tall guys. Whenever a tall male stands next to me, I step away for no reason. Also, every guy I've had a crush on has been short, some of them even shorter than me! I realized this about a year ago. The other thing that doesn't make sense is that I'm scared of water. I don't like to go on boats or swim. In fact even the beach freaks me out. I believe that I have these feelings because of my past life. Maybe a tall man drowned me? It sounds creepy, but I don't know what else to think! "

guard-ian angel

❝ I was in the mall parking lot walking to my car when a man approached me and told me to drop my purse. I did what he said, and then a security guard came out and started yelling at the man. The guy got spooked and ran away. The guard asked me if I was okay, and I glanced at his badge and saw that his name was Mark. I told him I was fine and then bent down to pick up my purse.

ghostly encounter

When I stood up to thank him, he was gone. I was pretty shaken up, so I went back inside to the security booth to tell them what had happened. When I said that Mark had helped me, the guard in the booth said that I must have been mistaken because the last Mark to work there had died six months earlier! He said I probably misread his badge, but I know what I saw, and I know that Mark was there for me that night—at least in spirit!"

that's the spirit

"My parents had always told me of a friendly ghost that followed our family around. Well, one night I was lying in bed at around three in the morning. My door was open, so I could see directly into the living room. I'd just woken up and happened to glance out the door. When I did, I saw this little old man sitting on the couch staring at me! I pulled the covers over my head, and when I went to peek again he was gone. Needless to say, I ran to my parents' room screaming! Now, as a 19-year-old, I've had several encounters with the ghost, and I've come to accept the man as my guardian angel of sorts—always there in the background watching out for me and my family."

child psych-ology

" There's this little lane that winds through the woods behind my grandmother's house. I have a recurring dream that I'm walking down the lane and I come to a door. I walk through the door, but I always wake up before I find out where it goes. So one day, I was at my grandmother's house baby-sitting my 4-year-old cousin. We were walking down the little lane when out of the blue my cousin asked, 'Where's the door?' I looked at him in shock because I know I've never told anyone about that dream! It still freaks me out to think about it. **"**

extra freaky

lucy in the sky

" I was at home helping my mom clean up the living room. There was an *I Love Lucy* rerun playing on TV, and we were just listening and laughing. My mom is a huge *I Love Lucy* fan and even has a photo of Lucille Ball and Desi Arnaz hanging in the kitchen. Well, as we were cleaning, my mom said, 'That Lucy was just the best actress out there!' At that moment, we heard this huge crash in the kitchen. We ran in and the picture of Lucy and Desi was lying on the kitchen counter. So weird! "

camera man

" I was home alone because my mom was at work and my sister was out with her friends. I was bored, so I decided to test out my new Web camera. I was being weird, just goofing off and taking pictures of myself. After a few dozen shots, I went through each one to see if I wanted to save it or delete it. After laughing at some of them, I found a picture I definitely could not laugh at. Behind me there was a blur that looked like the figure of a man with shoulder-length hair. I freaked out and ran away from the computer. When my sister came home, I showed her the picture, and she thought I'd Photoshopped it! A lot of people thought the figure was my sister because of the hair. I still have the picture, and yet I have no idea what it really was! Now, whenever I take a picture, I always look behind me to make sure there is nothing there. **"**

midnight run

" My dad was taking my mom to the airport, and I decided to come along too. It was around 4 o'clock in the morning, and I was sleeping in the backseat of the car. After about 15 minutes, I got up and looked out the window, and I saw the strangest thing: It looked like a figure of a guy in his mid-30s jogging next to us on the highway with his golden retriever. I was thinking about how impossible it was for a man to be jogging at 70 miles per hour, but before I could really take in what was happening, he disappeared! "

angel eyes

"My cousin and his wife had just had a baby, Michael, when weird stuff started to happen. Every night, they'd rock Michael to sleep in a rocking chair on the opposite side of the room from his crib, but when they'd come back the next morning, the chair would be right next to the crib. And Michael always looks around the room and laughs—at nothing. Finally, whenever they'd take a picture of him, there would be a halo of sparkles around him, like the camera was out of focus, but the rest of the picture would be in focus! One day, our grandma said, 'Michael must have a special angel with him.' We all laughed at first, but maybe it's true!"

night vision

" A couple summers ago, I had this vivid dream that I was in school and I was presenting a project with a girl I'd never seen before. In my dream, I kept calling the girl Stephanie, and we ended up getting a B on the report. Well, I forgot about the dream until the next year. A new girl named Stephanie started at our school, and we got paired for a project. I finally remembered my dream, but I didn't want her to think I was weird, so I only told her about it after we got our grade back—a B! "

fly girl

" A couple of years ago, I had a really crazy experience. My mom randomly asked me if I remembered getting out of my crib and crawling into her room one time when I was a baby. Apparently, no one knew how I could have gotten out of my crib—and they were baffled. When my mom asked that, I suddenly did remember what happened back then. It was like it was a movie replaying in my mind. One night, I was standing up in my crib and I tried to jump out—but instead, I floated over the bar and onto the floor like a feather and crawled into my parents' room. I didn't tell my mom what I remembered because I didn't want to freak her out, but I will always wonder if that's what really happened that night. ”

extreme makeover

" I was dreaming that I had a nose like Michael Jackson's. I woke up and looked in the mirror and the hair on the back of my neck stood up. I had chills. I could've sworn my nose had changed—but it hadn't. I was so freaked out that I would have to go around looking like Michael! "

double trouble

" I have this really weird connection with my best friend, Nicole. We lead parallel lives and even get hurt at the same time!

psychic powers

For instance, last spring break I was in Miami, and I fell off the bed and broke my wrist. The exact same day, Nicole fell off a scooter back home and broke her wrist. Then, a year later, Nicole was rushed to the hospital one night to have her appendix removed. Who was there? Me! I had been rushed to the hospital an hour earlier to get my appendix removed! We've always said we're connected by some strong cosmic force, and now everyone else is starting to believe us! "

snow angel

" A few years ago, I was in an accident on a secluded road during a blizzard. I was thrown through the windshield, and I couldn't move and was in and out of consciousness. When I woke up in the hospital, I asked the doctor how I got there. He said that my mother, Bethany, brought me in and left. He had never seen us before, so he couldn't have known that she'd been dead for four years! I don't know what really happened, but it seems like my mother is an angel—and she saved my life that day. "

dream work

" I always keep a journal beside my bed so I can write down my dreams as soon as I wake up if I still remember them. One day last summer, I was talking to my friend Brittany on the phone, and we were discussing phone numbers. For some reason, I was looking through my dream journal from January of last year while we were on the phone, and as I was paging through it, I came across a dream I had with a phone number in it.

Well, because of our conversation, I decided to tell Brittany all about my phone number dream. Then, just to be funny, I read her the number. When she heard all the digits, she was just like, 'What?! That's Marc's number!' It turns out that the phone number in my dream was actually the same one her boyfriend Marc had—and they'd just met in May. Brittany didn't even know who he was back then when I had that dream! **"**

floored!

" One day I was alone in this really slow elevator at a hotel when all of a sudden, I heard something whisper, 'Hello.' I got so scared. I closed my eyes and held my breath until the elevator got to my floor and the doors opened! For the rest of my stay there I took the stairs! "

teen wolf

" For the longest time I was having dreams that I was a big, white wolf. Even when I am wide awake, I can see things through a wolf's eyes. Plus, I seem to be able to sense when someone is bad news, and I often react to certain things just as a wolf would. Like, when I'm cornered or frightened, I get mad and lash out. I know it probably sounds silly, but I think that I must have been a wolf in a past life. "

flash forward

psychic powers

" Last year, I was out eating dinner at a restaurant with a couple of my guy friends on a stormy fall night. The whole time we were out, I felt a little 'off' and kept getting the shivers——I just had this feeling that something bad was going to happen, but I didn't want to tell anyone about it. The storm was getting worse, and the lightning fiercer, so one of the guys said he'd bring the car around. But before he went to get it, I told him to wait. He kind of blew me off, saying he wanted to get the car before the rain got so bad that we wouldn't be able to drive home. But as he opened the door, I jumped in front of him and, for some reason, screamed, 'No! Don't go outside!' Well, just then, an enormous bolt of lightning hit the restaurant sign right above us, causing an explosion of fire and electric bolts. My friend jumped back quickly and turned around, looking at me with fear and disbelief in his eyes. Who knows how badly the lightning would've injured him if he'd been hit? He could have died. Now he always tells people I saved his life! **"**

sign from above

"I have asthma, so I sometimes have attacks. Well, I had just moved into my new house; it was only the fifth night that we had lived there. Before I went to bed I had a hard time breathing, as though an asthma attack was coming on. I was starting to freak out but I didn't want to wake my parents up, so I just got my inhaler and did my breathing exercises. Eventually, I fell asleep. But when I woke up the next morning, a cross was lying next to me, as if to protect me from an attack. I had hung it above my door the day we moved into the house. I told my family the story—we were all spooked! "

defensive dreamer

"One night I had this really weird dream. In it my dad was taking me and my best friend to school, but he dropped us off at the local truck stop because he said he didn't have enough time. I went inside to call someone to pick us up. But when I walked in, a lady dressed all in black said I couldn't make the call. I looked over my shoulder and there was a funeral service for an old man going on. I woke up after that. The next day my sister, who works at the truck stop in real life, had to go to work on her day off. The man who was supposed to work that day had died the night before!"

table dancing

"One night during a thunderstorm I was sleeping over at my friend's house. She was in the basement getting soda while I was in the dining room finding sheets to sleep on. Her family was moving in a few days, and all the boxes were in there along with the dining room table and chairs. Then the power went out for a second, and when it came back on the chairs were on the table! The light went back out, then on again, and everything was normal. It was like something out of a horror movie. I'm so glad they moved out of that house!"

nirvana drama

" At my drama camp, we stayed in college dorms that were supposedly haunted. One night, this girl held a séance to call back Kurt Cobain. We sat in a circle, she lit a candle and put the match in a puddle on the table, and we began chanting, 'Kurt Cobain, give us a sign.' After the fifth chant, we noticed the candle starting to flicker. Then we saw the match on the table light up again. Some of the girls yelled, and we all stopped holding hands, so we never officially closed the circle. That night, I woke up to the closet door opening, and as I sat up, it slammed shut. I know we released something not quite right that night, but it wasn't Kurt. "

copy cat

" A couple of months after my dog Ernie died, I found a kitten hiding on our porch. She scared me at first, so I named her Boo. Boo had the same behaviors as Ernie—she liked to lie in his favorite spot, her favorite place to be petted was the same as his, and she meowed at the same times Ernie would bark. Boo really helped me cope with Ernie's death. After a year, she just left and never came back. I think Boo was Ernie's way of letting me know he was still watching over me. "

mystery guest

" I baked some cookies for the new neighbors who had moved in down the hall from me, but nobody was home when I brought them over, so I left them on a tray by the door with a note. The next day, a woman named Sarah Rees came to thank me and asked for the recipe, and I wrote it down for her. It called for sugar, but Sarah didn't have any and asked if she could borrow some. I said yes and went to get it for her. But when I turned back around, she was gone, and the tray and recipe were on the floor. The next day, I went over to see what happened, but nobody answered. I tried knocking a few more times over the next few days, but no one was ever there. A week later, I cleaned my closet and found old newspapers from 1992. On one, in big print, it said that a Sarah Rees died in a car accident right outside our building!"

twist of date

" My family has a cabin on a lake in Washington that we visit every summer. The cabin used to belong to my great-grandpa, but now it's my uncle's. One day, my uncle, my sister, and I were cleaning out the chimney, and we found this cement plate that none of us had ever seen before. It had my great-grandpa's name carved in it. The weird thing was that when we cleaned it, we saw the date August 3, 1953, inscribed on it—and it was August 3, 2003. We found the plate on exactly the same day—just 50 years later! "

mummy dearest

" I've been having dreams about ancient Egypt. In one of my dreams I gave birth to six children. Then one day in class we were learning about Queen Nefertiti. The teacher asked us how many children Nefertiti had with her husband. I blanked out and no one knew the answer, but suddenly I thought of my dream and blurted out, 'Six kids.' The teacher looked up and said that I was correct. So I think I might have been Queen Nefertiti in a past life! "

spirit dancer

" I was crushed when I didn't get into drama school, so I went to mope in the park. This old lady sat next to me, and we started talking. She told me she'd wanted to be a ballerina—but after a bad experience, she gave up, and she'd always regretted it. I walked her home, and the next day, I went back to her house to tell her I'd decided not to give up on my dream. But the young woman who opened the door said that no old lady had lived there for at least 10 years! "

offensive driver

" My mom died when she was hit by a drunk driver. The driver lived, but he's currently in jail. Ever since then, I've had dreams where the driver comes up to me and asks me all these freaky questions. On the one-year anniversary of my mom's death, my dad and I were at her grave when he remembered he left his car lights on. While he was gone, this guy came up to me and started asking all these odd questions. It was so weird—he was just like the drunk driver in my dream. But since he was in jail, I knew it couldn't have been him. Or could it? **"**

sign language

" A year ago, my mom died of breast cancer. One day, I was at my sister's old apartment helping her pack up to move, and I cut my knee on a shelf. It started to bleed, so I put on a Band-Aid and just forgot about it. Then, getting out of the shower a few days later, I noticed the Band-Aid had fallen off. I looked at the mark from my cut—and it was the exact shape of the breast cancer ribbon. I knew no one would believe me, so I showed my sister and my dad. They were both in shock—that day was the one-year anniversary of my mom's death. I like to think it was a funny little sign from her. "

hex files

" When my mom was five months pregnant with my younger brother Kevin, she and I were sitting in our car in the Pizza Hut parking lot, waiting for our pizza to be ready, when a scary-looking woman knocked on her window. My mom rolled it down a tiny bit, and the woman asked what time it was. Mom told her the time and then closed the window again. Well, then the woman tried to get in the car, but luckily, the doors were locked. So she walked back to my mom's window and started reciting a bunch of weird chants and screaming about a baby. Then she bent down, picked up a pinecone, and bit into it! That night, my mom was rushed to the hospital with stomach pains and had to have surgery to save her pregnancy. Fortunately, my brother was okay, but we're convinced that we almost lost him to a voodoo curse! **"**

mystery meat

" At my grandfather's funeral, my uncle said he wished he could bring him one last cheeseburger since that was his all-time favorite food. After the burial, we all went out to eat, and when the waitress brought out our food, we somehow ended up with an extra cheeseburger that no one had ordered! Obviously, there's no way that she could have known what my uncle had said, so we think it was a hello from my grandpa in heaven. **"**

electric company

" I was playing online when I got a message from guardianangel4u. It said, 'Don't use the pencil sharpener at school tomorrow in English class.' I just thought it was a prank. But the next day, in the middle of a huge English test, my pencil broke, and when I went to use the sharpener, I remembered the message. So just to be safe, I asked the teacher if I could borrow a pencil instead. That afternoon, a person used the sharpener, got a bad electric shock, and ended up in the hospital. I went back online and looked for guardianangel4u, but that user name didn't exist! My 'guardian angel' saved me! "

play thing

" My mom has this porcelain doll named Amanda in her room, and it has always creeped me out. One time my best friend and I were in my mom's room watching TV and the Amanda doll was sitting on a table facing the window. The first time I looked over at the doll, it was still facing the window. But when I looked again a few minutes later it was staring at me! I screamed and my friend freaked out and screamed too! Now every time I'm in the room with Amanda I turn her so she faces the wall...and pray that she won't turn around. "

window shopping

" I had this dream once about a window that showed you the one person who was meant for you. I looked in it and saw a guy. He didn't seem familiar, so in my dream, I asked someone what his name was, and she said, 'Kevin.' When I woke up the next morning, I didn't think anything of it. But that night, I went out with my friends and ended up meeting the hottest guy. Guess what his name was? Kevin! I was instantly hooked. We're so in love now, and I still think of that dream and get chills! "

large bookcase that had belonged to my mother. It was exactly like the one in my dream. I went to the third shelf, and sure enough, there was a piece of paper. It was an entry from the diary she kept when I was a baby. She had written about how much she loved me and how she couldn't wait to watch me grow up. That dream must've been her way of directing me to her wonderful note. **"**

scaredy cat

" We have three cats in our house. One time, I was walking to the bathroom when one of the cats ran under my feet and tripped me. He was gone before I could see him, but I yelled, 'You stupid cat!' My mom heard and asked what was wrong. So I told her one of our cats had just tripped me. She said, 'You're crazy—all three cats have been sitting in bed with me for the last hour.' Weird, right?! Guess we have a ghost cat too! "

holy roller

" I live in this house that's been around since 1745. The person who lived there before us was a priest from the church across the street. After he died, we moved in. One day, my little sister was playing with a toy car on the front lawn. She had left all her dolls in the house, so she put a priest figurine that she always carried in her pocket in the driver's seat (we're sort of a religious family). Well, the car rolled all the way across the lawn, across the street, and into the church parking lot—but we don't live on a hill, and the car doesn't have a remote control or anything! We threw that car away immediately. "

double vision

" I was home alone, and I wanted to go swimming. On my way to grab a towel, I went by my little sister's room and saw her on the floor playing Barbies. I just walked by—but then I remembered that she was at her friend's house! I ran back to her room, but no one was there. Later, I told my mom and sister about it, and my sister said, 'Well, one time when you were sleeping, I went to the bathroom and left the door open— and then I saw myself walk by!' My mom and I just sat there in shock! "

news clues

"I thought my attic was haunted, so one day, my sister and I decided to go up and explore. She held the door open, and we both sat on the steps. All of a sudden, we heard a rustling noise and a thump. My sister screamed, and then it felt like someone was pushing us away. We slammed the door, ran out of there, and went downstairs to calm down for a while. A little later, we decided to go back up again. It turns out that an old newspaper had fallen off a shelf. But guess what the headline was? 'Missing Body Found Under Attic Floorboards'! I'll never ever go up there again!"

the name game

" My boyfriend Austin and I had been going out for almost a year when I had a dream: I was walking down this street and all of a sudden, a person appeared in the shadows and asked if I knew Austin. I said yes, and then she told me I should ask him about Lauren. That's when I woke up. I didn't know anyone named Lauren, but the next day, when I asked Austin about her, he got really nervous and said, 'Who told you about her?' Then he totally exploded at me for spying on him. Later on, I found out he'd been cheating on me for a month with some girl named Lauren. I don't know who sent me that supernatural message, but I'm sure glad they did. "

dead end street

" My family was driving home on this long, dark street. There was a lady in the middle of the road who had short hair and was wearing a white skirt. Her car was on the side of the road with all the doors open, the lights on, and the music turned up really loud. My dad stopped to ask if she needed help, and she started crying and said she was waiting for someone but thanked him anyway. So he took off, and when I turned around to look at her again, she was gone! There's no way she could've left so fast. The next day on the news, they said that on that same street, a lady was stabbed to death while waiting by the side of the road after getting a flat tire—two nights earlier! "

smoke signal

" Last summer, my grandmother died of lung cancer. She had been living with us, and she'd usually go out for a smoke before she went to bed, around 3 a.m. Two weeks after she died, our house alarm went off around 3 a.m. My dad checked the alarm, and it showed that it had been set off by an opened door—the one leading from my grandmother's room to the outside. Before we go to bed each night, he always locks all the doors and closes the blinds, but when we went into her room, the sliding glass door was halfway open. It had been unlocked— from the inside! I won't be moving into that room anytime soon! "

swing lesson

❝ I was in the woods with my neighbor, swinging from a tree at the top of a cliff. I accidentally let go and went soaring face first toward the rocky side of the cliff. I was sure I was going to die, but then I felt something or someone push my legs. My whole body turned, and I landed on all fours—without a scratch. Crazy! ❞

off the wall

" I was staying the night at my friend's house, and we were bored. We had a few bottles of glow-in-the-dark paint, and we decided to splash it on the walls of her bedroom and turn on her black light. We'd been doing that for awhile when all of a sudden, the paint started dripping down the wall, forming the shape of a woman. There was no way we were imagining it. We could see her hair and the side of her face, both of her legs, everything! She appeared to have her arms pressed up against the wall, like she was trying to escape or break free. We freaked and ran out of the room. I haven't been back there since! **"**

message board

" When I was little, I had an idea to name my daughter Somorra. I used to draw pictures of her with long black hair because that's what I thought she would look like. I never told anyone though. Then when I was 13, I was over at my cousin's house, and I fell asleep on the couch while she was playing with a Ouija board on the floor with her friend. When I woke up, I asked if they had any luck contacting spirits, and they said, 'Yeah, we met a girl named Somorra. She said she had long black hair, and you would meet her when you are 23.' I froze. They couldn't possibly have known about her—it had to be my future daughter! **"**

all shook up

" I was spending the night at my friend's house when she started talking in her sleep. It was funny at first, until she started shouting, 'Help me, Kelsey' over and over and shaking violently. I was so freaked out, I tried shaking her and yelled, 'I'm here! What do you want?!' That's when she sat up, grabbed my throat, and said, 'I want you dead, Kelsey.' I screamed and turned on the lights, and she flopped on her back and was silent again. I shook her, and this time she woke up for real and got mad at me for waking her up! I haven't slept over since! "

auto insurance

❝ A year ago, my best friend Krystal died from cancer. One night, I was baby-sitting, waiting for the parents to get home, when I heard footsteps on the stairs. I figured it was one of the kids, so I went to see what they wanted. But when I got to the stairs, it wasn't the kids—it was Krystal. She told me in a quiet but serious voice, 'Don't get in the car.'

ghostly encounter

Then she walked back up the stairs and disappeared. I was freaked! But later that week, I was at a party where kids were drinking. I was about to accept a ride home when I remembered Krystal's warning and quickly said no. Well, the people I was going to ride with had an accident and were all killed. It's awful, but I thank God every day for my guardian angel. "

feeling alien-ated

"One night, my family and I were watching TV when all of a sudden the power went out. Then the house got super hot, so we went outside for some air. As we were standing on the porch, I got a funny feeling something weird was about to happen. Just then, I looked up at the sky and saw a bolt of colorful light flash across. It was so low down it almost seemed to touch our roof. As soon as it was gone, it got very cold and the power went back on. I know it was a UFO. I definitely believe in them now."

blank screen

" Once during a boring movie, I decided to let my mind go blank and let random thoughts pop up. Suddenly, I felt a knot in my stomach and heard the words 'Something is wrong with Bill.' Bill is my parents' friend (I never think about him). I let it go until after the movie, and then I called home. My mom was crying—Bill had been rushed to the hospital! I dropped my phone and started to shake. I don't 'let my mind go blank' anymore! "

roundabout nightmare

" I have frequent dreams about being a blond boy who's around 16 or 18 years old, living in London sometime during the last century. I also have nightmares about being in his body and dying in a horrific car crash where his head gets crushed after the car rolls upside down. I think that I was him in my past life because I've woken up many times right after the dream with an intense, sharp throbbing in my head. **"**

van-ishing point

" My mom and I were driving on a busy road when a young couple in the next car over smiled at us. Just then they slammed into the car in front of them that was waiting to pull into a parking lot. We tried to look back, but we couldn't see anything. We kept saying that we had to know if they were alive or not. That's when a white van cut in front of my mom—and it had a license plate that said 'alive' on it. My mom and I looked at each other in shock. When we looked again, the van was gone. But there was nowhere to turn off—it's as though it just completely vanished! "

hello, kitty!

" I once owned a cat named Nickey who was like a sister to me. Anytime I was sad, she seemed to know and would cuddle with me until I was all right. But she got hit and killed by a car—I was so upset! One night, I was crying about it in my computer room when this little electronic kitty toy I had came alive for a few seconds, and then stopped. But my baby sister had trashed that toy, and it didn't have batteries in it! I was freaked, but I also felt warm inside because I had a sense that it was Nickey saying that things would be okay. "

car alarm

" I had a recurring dream about a car in flames on an overpass, and I'd wake up with a feeling of fear in the pit of my stomach. Then one day, we were driving to visit my grandmother when the sky went dark, and it began to pour. All of a sudden, a familiar-looking car passed us, and I got that feeling of fear from my dream. 'Dad, pull over!' I screamed. He thought something was wrong with me so he did. That car neared the overpass ahead, and next thing you know, it collided full speed with another car and then burst into flames. Once my dream came true, I never had it again! **"**

186

wall flowers

" A while ago, my boyfriend had cheated on me, and I was so frustrated because I never knew who the girl was. One night in my room, I just said to myself, 'I need a sign. I have to know who my boyfriend cheated on me with.' As I said it, a bouquet of dried flowers that had been hanging on my wall since our one-year anniversary fell. I was so freaked, I called my best friend to tell her. And you know what she said? 'That's weird, because the flowers I kept from my sister's wedding fell off my shelf right before you called.' I took that as a sign that it was her! I hung up on her immediately, and things haven't been the same since. "

double doors

" When I was little, if I woke up in the middle of the night, I'd go sleep in my parents' bed. I didn't want to wake them, so I would just lie on the corner near my dad and fall back asleep. Every time I did that, I would have the same dream: These hooded men (like monks) would pick me up by my arms and legs and drag me down to my basement, where they'd open this little door and throw me in a dark room. Then I'd wake up in the morning back in my own bed. Obviously, it was my dad carrying me back to my room that made me have that dream. But many years later, we did some construction in the basement, and when we broke through one of the walls, we found a tiny door hidden behind it! Now, how could I have known about that?!"

pushy kids

ghostly encounter

" My friends and I heard a story about an old slaughterhouse where some kids were killed. The rumor was that if you drove up, turned your car around, and put it in neutral, it would move. Then if you put powder on the bumper, you'd see tiny fingerprints. We had to try it! In a few seconds, the car moved a good 20 feet uphill until we slammed on the brakes. When we shined a light on the bumper, there were fingerprints on it. I've done it several times, and it always happens. The story is that the kids who died there are pushing you away. "

pass it on

"My uncle and I were the best of buddies, so when he passed away four years ago, I was pretty devastated. About a month ago, I had a dream: I was baby-sitting in an old house when all of a sudden, this door opens with a cold breeze, and a bright light shines out. I walk into the room, and my uncle's sitting there. I sit next to him, and he says, 'She won't listen to me.' And then the dream ends. I told my mom the next day, and she called her sister (my uncle's wife) to tell her about it. My aunt wasn't really surprised. She said, 'I know he's been trying to talk to me, but I'm trying to let go of him and move on!'"

ball-istic

" My friend and I were cleaning my room one day when I found this little red ball underneath my bed. Without really thinking, I threw it in the hallway and shut the door behind me. About 20 minutes later, we heard a noise coming from the hallway. I opened the door and saw the ball bouncing up and down as if someone were standing there dribbling it like a basketball! Since nobody else was home and my friend was in my room the entire time, I have no idea what—or who—made the ball do that. "

shocker room

" I was at a high school across town for a basketball game. Just as I got on the bus to go home, I realized I'd forgotten my jacket in the locker room, so I ran back to get it. It was dark inside, and I was searching for my jacket when a girl walked in and pointed to a bench. My jacket was on the bench, so I thanked her, grabbed it, and left. As I ran out of the school, I saw a big plaque on the wall—a memorial to a student who had died three years before. There was a picture of the girl I'd just seen in the locker room! I still get chills whenever I have a basketball game at that school! "

ghostly encounter

card trick

" Last April, my brother got a card in the mail. My mom was shocked because the writing on the envelope looked just like her mother's (my grandmother's), who had been dead for over six years. He opened it and gasped—it was a Christmas card from my grandmother! The postmark was 1996, three months before she died, but the card came in 2002! Then, three weeks later, I opened a brand-new book, and a faded bookmark fell out with my grandmother's name written on the back. But no one had ever opened the book before me! "

sleep disorder

extra freaky

" For a long time, I've had these scary experiences at night. As I'm drifting off to sleep, I suddenly get paralyzed, and a sensation of doom surrounds me. My head and chest feel like they're being crushed, and I try to scream, but no matter how hard I try, I can't! I've researched it, and there are a lot of different theories—I believe it's a devil sitting on me. If I'm lucky, my sister (who I sleep with for this very purpose!) feels me moving, and she'll shake me awake. It's like being trapped! I know I'm not the only one to experience this, but that's not very comforting. **"**

hand sign

" I've studied Wicca for two years. One night, at my friend's house, we felt a presence in the room. So we lit a candle, but it went out after only 30 seconds, even though the window was shut. Then my friend screamed, and I looked down to see a tiny handprint on my shoulder. It didn't fade for 20 minutes! That night, I had horrible visions of a fire and children screaming. We researched her house and found out that in the 1920s, when the first house was built on her property, a man had set a fire that killed him and his whole family! The day the handprint appeared was the same date as the fire! "

sea spirit

ghostly encounter

" I was having dinner with my family and a friend at a restaurant that's in a 100-year-old building. As we ate, my dad told us about a ghost that supposedly haunts the building. I didn't believe him, so we asked our waitress about it. She said that about 75 years ago, a huge hurricane hit the area. There was a mandatory evacuation, but one woman stayed behind anyway. The building ended up flooding, and the woman was eventually swept out to sea. The waitress told us that her body was never found and that her spirit haunts the building—and now the restaurant—today. I was still a little skeptical, but then my friend pointed out that her glass of water, which she'd only taken one sip from, was completely empty! When the waitress came back, she told us that the ghost does that sometimes. I became a believer right then and there! **"**

hair raiser

“ I had a dream that my grandma got in a fight with my mom because they had the same haircut. But in my dream, Grandma had a blue van that I'd never seen before. The next day, my mom had her hair cut short, and I said, 'Remember when Grandma had that blue van, and you and she had that same haircut?' (I must have thought the dream was a memory.) My mom looked at me weird and said, 'I remember that, but you weren't even born yet!' It just completely freaked me out right there! ”

red-y for love

" My mom started having these really weird dreams about events that haven't happened yet but usually come true. One night she had a dream that the next guy I fell in love with would have red hair and would be wearing a red shirt when I met him. Two weeks later, my older sister had a baby. I went to the hospital to see her and gasped when I walked in. She was holding her newborn son—she had put him in a red nightgown and he had little tufts of bright red hair on his head. I guess my mother was right—he was the next guy I fell in love with! "

space invader

" My sister and I were alone in our house—she was upstairs drying her hair, and I was downstairs watching TV. Suddenly, I heard her yell into our bedroom (it's around the corner from our bathroom), 'Why did you unplug my hair dryer?' I went upstairs, and my sister looked completely freaked to see me! She said that her hair was flipped upside down, so she couldn't see, and all of a sudden, the dryer stopped. The door had opened just enough for someone to slip their hand in and unplug it. When she went into the hall, she saw the shadow of a person walk into our room. But I was downstairs! "

cause for alarm

extra freaky

"My grandmother had a brain aneurysm and was in the intensive care unit. Before she passed away, my mom and I asked her to give us a sign that she was okay once she'd 'crossed over.' Minutes after she died, the fire alarm went off. When the firefighters came to check it out, they said the alarm had been set off from my grandma's room—but there was no sign of smoke or fire. My mom and I knew that setting off the alarm was her way of telling us she was okay."

father figure

" One day I was in the basement, chatting online with friends. After about two hours, my stepdad came downstairs and yelled at me for tying up the phone line. Then he turned around and went upstairs. At the exact moment he walked out, the phone rang. My stepdad was on the phone and said he had just gotten in a car accident. I was confused and said that was impossible—I just saw him. He said he was miles from home. "

thank-you note

" When my dad's friend Beau suddenly died, my parents volunteered to clean out his office. After packing everything up, they took the boxes out to their car. Then they went back inside to lock up, and my mom noticed a sticky note on the wall that read, 'Thank you, Roe'—which is my dad's name. My parents told me they could feel Beau's presence, and they just sat there in silence for a while before leaving. Now, months later, my dad still can't bring himself to go back into that office. "

index

a

Aliens, 63, 180
Angels, 30–31, 119, 126,
    133, 157, 178–179,
    194
Arena man, 64–65
Art, moving, 84–85, 101,
    175
Asthma, cross protection,
    140
Attic, haunted, 168

b

Ball, bouncing, 193
Ballerina, 151
Bathroom sink taps,
    26–27, 107
Birds, 72–73, 103
Boyfriends, 32, 135, 160,
    169, 187

c

Camp, 50, 76, 144
Car alarm, 186
Card trick, 195
Carpet footprints, 111
Cars, 16, 22, 125, 152,
    161, 178–179, 183,
    190, 204
Car, toy, 165
Cats, 12, 17, 145, 164,
    185
Computer, 71, 122–123
Contacts, 100

d

Daughter, vision of, 176
Death experience, 114
Dice doubles, 9
Doll, Native American, 95
Doll, porcelain, 159
Doorbell, 97
Double vision, 167
Dreams and nightmares
    African princess, 77
    being grabbed, 39, 55
    being stabbed, 67
    of death, 141
    dream boys, 14–15,
        160, 201
    fairy handprints, 13
    mother's killer, 152
    mysterious doors,
        188–189
    night dive, 33

nose, 130
note from dead mother, 162–163
past lives, 61, 149, 182
phone number in, 134–135
plane crash, 82
recurring dream, 120
visions, 14–15, 127, 160, 200
wedding crasher, 32

e

Elevators, 11, 136
Extra freaky, 12, 92–93, 100, 114, 120, 161, 177, 196, 203

f

Fire, sign of, 197
Floating baby, 128–129
Flower vase, 46–47
Furniture, moving, 104–105, 143

g

Ghostly encounters, 16, 32, 42–43, 56, 88–89, 96, 98–99, 108–109, 116–117, 119, 146–147, 170–171, 178–179, 190, 194, 198–199
Glow-in-the-dark paint woman, 175
Golden light, man in, 52–53

h

Hair dryer mystery, 202

i

Instant messenger, 91

k

Knocks on wall, 90

l

Locket protector, 161

m

'Magic' bracelet, 29
Mailbox, 49
Marbles, 75
Milk, sister wanting, 78–79
Mirror, girl in, 57
Murderer, 25
Music box, 21

n

Noises in house, 41, 44,
46–47, 112–113

p

Past lives, 12, 61, 77, 87,
115, 137, 149, 182
Psychic powers, 22, 37,
51, 106, 131, 138–139,
141, 181, 186, 201

q

Queen Nefertiti, 149

r

Relatives, dead
aunt, 95
best friend, 178–179
brother, 26–27, 35
father, 12, 36, 92–93
grandfather, 18–19, 23,
69, 92–93, 156
grandmother, 83,
98–99, 103, 172, 195
mother, 92–93, 152,
153, 162–163
uncle, 21, 58–59, 191
Romanov, Maria, 61

s

Sea spirit, 198–199
Shocks, 114, 116–117,
138–139, 157
Shower radio, 66
Sleep, paralysis before,
196
Sleep, talking in, 117
Sleep walking, 81
Smoke alarms, 35, 203

t

Tea sets, 23, 28
Thank-you note, from other
side, 205
Trains, 16
Tree, swinging from, 173
TV, 8, 36, 96, 121

v

Van, vanishing, 183
Voice, warning from, 70
Voodoo curse, 154–155

w

Window, people in, 40, 45,
56
Wolf, 137